THE
JUKEBOX MAN

JACQUELINE K. OGBURN · *pictures by* JAMES RANSOME

Dial Books for Young Readers New York

Published by Dial Books for Young Readers
A member of Penguin Putnam Inc.
375 Hudson Street
New York, New York 10014

Text copyright © 1998 by Jacqueline K. Ogburn
Pictures copyright © 1998 by James E. Ransome
All rights reserved
Designed by Atha Tehon
Printed in Hong Kong
First Edition
1 3 5 7 9 10 8 6 4 2

Library of Congress Cataloging in Publication Data
Ogburn, Jacqueline K.
The jukebox man/Jacqueline K. Ogburn;
pictures by James Ransome.—1st ed.
p.   cm.
Summary: After watching her grandfather repair
broken jukeboxes and change records at diners, restaurants, fish camps,
and truck stops, a little girl dances with him to her favorite tune.
ISBN 0-8037-1429-7 (trade).—ISBN 0-8037-1430-0 (lib. bdg.)
[1. Grandfathers—Fiction. 2. Jukeboxes—Fiction.]
I. Ransome, James E., ill. II. Title.
PZ7.03317 Ju   1998 [E]—dc20   95-40281   CIP AC

The illustrations were done in oils on paper.

In memory of my grandfathers—

W. E. Jack Ogburn, Sr.

and

G. L. Jack Bost

J. K. O.

For Jackie Ogburn.
Thanks for all your help in bringing
this book to light.

J. E. R.

Poppaw was a jukebox man. He had jukeboxes in dozens of diners and restaurants, fish camps and truck stops all over the state. He would make the rounds, changing the records, fixing the machines, and splitting the take with the owners. One Saturday he came by the house to take me with him.

"Up you go, Pumpkin," he said, lifting me onto the seat of his pickup truck. "You take care of my keys, now."

Poppaw kept his keys on a big ring attached to a long stick. He would thread the stick through his belt loop and the keys would jingle when he walked. The belt loop on my jeans was too small, so I had to hold tight to the stick and wave it to make the keys jingle.

We drove out of town, down a twisty little road in the woods to LeRoy's Fish Camp. It was a big pine building on the edge of a pond.

Poppaw carried the big box of records with his money and tools inside. I walked in front with the keys. The dining hall was cool and dim, with rows and rows of tables. It smelled like hot grease and fish and biscuits.

The jukebox was a grand Wurlitzer, the kind with a curved top and bubbles in the tubes of lights. "Keys, please," said Poppaw. Opening up the front, he checked the counters to see how many times the different selections were played. He took out the unpopular 45s and handed them to me to put back in the box. He changed the labels as he changed the records, making sure that everything was in the right place.

Then we pulled the machine away from the wall and Poppaw opened the cash box. "I'll hold the pouch," I said. He poured the coins out of the box in a noisy stream. I had never seen so many quarters, nickels, and dimes at once. The pouch got so heavy, I had to rest the bottom on the floor.

Then we locked up the jukebox and pushed it back in place.

"Can I play some music?" I asked.

"Sure, Pumpkin," Poppaw said. "What's your favorite song?"

"'Blue Suede Shoes!'"

"OK, that's B-six, this button right here." He held me up to see.

I dropped in a nickel and punched in my choice. With a whirr and a click the record fell into place, the lights started up, and the music began.

The voice of Elvis Presley sang out. I danced in the glow of the bubbling lights, wishing that my shoes were blue, instead of black and white. I danced to the song three more times while Poppaw and Mr. LeRoy divided up the take. They sat at an empty table, making stacks of coins and rolling them up in paper sleeves. The jukebox flashed red, yellow, and green, and I twisted away in the patches of light on the floor.

The next stop was the Knife and Fork Truck Stop off I-40. It was about 3:00 and the dining room was empty. Instead of a big gaudy machine, there were selection boxes at each booth.

Poppaw greeted the waitress as we went behind the counter to the kitchen where the record console was. The kitchen was hot and smelled of coffee, vinegar, and damp hamburger buns. We went to work, changing the records while the cook chopped up cabbages for coleslaw. One of the records Poppaw took out was "Blue Suede Shoes." He handed it to me, saying, "Here's your favorite. Take it on home and dance all you want." I threaded the record onto the stick of keys and jingled them.

Poppaw gave me a quarter to play some music while he settled the money, but I didn't want to hear anything except "Blue Suede Shoes," and there were no lights to dance to here. So I sat on a stool at the counter and swiveled my hips from side to side while trying to keep my shoulders facing the counter.

"Well, hey there, honey," said the waitress. "Are you done helping your granddaddy? It sure is hot, would you like a soft drink? A Dr Pepper or a Sun-drop, maybe?"

"Yes, ma'am. A Dr Pepper, please." I showed her my quarter.

"You keep that money, now, we don't need to take anything from Jack's grandbaby. You like lots of ice? I always like lots of ice on a hot day, but don't chew on it, now, it'll crack your teeth," she said as she brought me a tall glass.

"No, ma'am, I won't. Thank you, ma'am," I said.

"Such sweet manners. You favor your daddy, he used to come here with Jack and he had sweet manners too. You are just as cute as a little june bug."

I did not think that I looked like a june bug. June bugs are fat and green and not cute at all. Fortunately two truck drivers came in, and the lady went to wait on them.

Soon Poppaw was ready to go, and we walked past the big tractor-trailers to our truck.

"We're heading to our last stop, Pumpkin," Poppaw said. "We have to take the old Seeburg back to the shop."

We drove to a little diner at the edge of town. After we took the money out, Poppaw had to talk more with the owner. Since I couldn't dance here either, I sat in a booth and kicked the side of the seat.

Then I noticed a big boy in the next booth, watching me. I twirled my record on the key stick.

"What are all them keys?" he asked.

"These are jukebox keys," I said. "My granddaddy is the jukebox man and we're going to take this one back to his shop and fix it."

Poppaw and the owner were lifting the jukebox onto a hand truck. I went over to help, but Poppaw said, "You hold the door open for us."

I turned toward the door, but that boy was holding it open. He grinned at me as I followed the jukebox out. I helped push the box over to the pickup.

Poppaw's blue Chevy had a special tailgate that was also a lift. He lowered the tailgate to the ground and rolled the jukebox onto it.

"Can I ride up, Poppaw?" I asked.

"If you stand next to me and hold on," he said. Then with a loud hum, the tailgate lifted us and the jukebox level with the truck bed. I waved to the boy standing next to the door of the diner. Poppaw pushed the jukebox onto the truck bed and we tied it in securely. Poppaw hopped off the tailgate and I jumped down into his arms. Then he closed the gate with a bang.

When we got back in the cab, I asked, "Are we going home now?"

"First we have to take this jukebox back to my shop," he said. "Grandma's fixing dinner for everybody, and your folks should already be there." I was disappointed, because that meant I would have to wait until I went home that evening to play my new record.

Back at Poppaw's house my parents were just getting out of our car next to the garage. I waved to them as we drove by, heading for the machine shop out in back of the house.

Daddy came walking down the drive as Poppaw was backing up the truck into the bay of the shop. I hopped out of the truck and ran to him. "Look, Daddy. Poppaw gave me the 'Blue Suede Shoes' record."

"That's nice, Donna. You go inside while we unload the truck," Daddy said.

I went inside the shop. There were jukeboxes all along the walls, some of them open with parts all around. I climbed up on the stool to watch them unload the Seeburg.

Around and around I spun the record on my key stick, thinking about dancing in front of the lights. Daddy was backing up, trying to get the big machine settled in a corner, when the record went sailing off my stick and spinning across the floor.

Crunch! The wheel of the hand truck rolled over the record, breaking the black vinyl into slivers. "What was that?" Poppaw asked.

"Just some old record," Daddy said. He dusted off his hands. "I'll see you two back at the house." Then he left.

I stared at the crushed record on the floor, blinking hard. "I'll clean it up, Poppaw," I said. Carefully I picked up the pieces and placed them in the trash barrel. Now I would have to wait for the song to come on the radio to hear it again.

"Come over here, Pumpkin, and help me with this," Poppaw said. He was holding a big extension cord. "Now plug these two in here."

I pushed in the plugs, and a Rock-ola and two Wurlitzers lit up.

"Hit C-five on that one over there," Poppaw told me. I stood on tiptoe and pushed the button. I heard clicks and whirrs, and three jukeboxes began to play. The music started and I heard Elvis singing about those shoes.

I laughed and Poppaw smiled, and we danced in the patches of light as the jukeboxes flashed red, yellow, and green.